LLAMA

ROCKS THE
CRADLE OF CHAOS

JONATHAN STUTZMAN

Illustrated by **HEATHER FOX**

Henry Holt and Company New York

Henry Holt and Company, *Publishers since 1866*
Henry Holt® is a registered trademark of Macmillan Publishing Group, LLC
120 Broadway, New York, NY 10271 • mackids.com

Our books may be purchased in bulk for promotional, educational, or business use.
Please contact your local bookseller or the Macmillan Corporate and Premium Sales Department
at (800) 221-7945 ext. 5442 or by email at MacmillanSpecialMarkets@macmillan.com.

Library of Congress Cataloging-in-Publication Data
Names: Stutzman, Jonathan, author. | Fox, Heather, illustrator.
Title: Llama rocks the cradle of chaos / Jonathan Stutzman ; illustrated by Heather Fox. Description: First edition. |
New York : Henry Holt Books for Young Readers, 2022. | Audience: Ages 4–8. | Audience: Grades 2–3. |
Summary: Greedy Llama travels back in time to eat his marvelous birthday donut a second time, but a Baby Llama follows
him to the present, and soon his house is a chaos of cave llamas, barbarian bunnies, and Viking pigs.
Identifiers: LCCN 2021046209 | ISBN 9781250776761 (hardcover) Subjects: LCSH: Llamas—Juvenile fiction. | Time travel—
Juvenile fiction. | Humorous stories. | CYAC: Llamas—Fiction. | Time travel—Fiction. | Humorous stories. | LCGFT: Humorous fiction.
Classification: LCC PZ7.1.S798 Lq 2022 | DDC [E]—dc23 LC record available at https://lccn.loc.gov/2021046209

First edition, 2022
Book design by Neil Swaab
Printed in China by Hung Hing Off-set Printing Co. Ltd.,
Heshan City, Guangdong Province

ISBN 978-1-250-77676-1 (hardcover)

1   3   5   7   9   10   8   6   4   2

For Ariel and Evolet

—FOX & STUTZ

Long, long ago, Llama rocked the cradle of chaos.

YESTERDAY

Yesterday was Llama's birthday,
and Llama celebrated his
birthday how he always did:

surrounded by his best friends—
wearing his fanciest party hat and his
finest birthday suit, and dining lavishly
on a doughnut with extra sprinkles.

It is your birthday

It was delicious. Spectacular. Why it tasted so spectacular he didn't know, but it filled his tummy and it filled his thoughts. He could not think of anything else the rest of the day.

At topiary club, his desires took shape.

At science club, he found holes in every theory.

they would lead him down an epic
path of delicious destruction.

TODAY

Today, Llama decided to
make his dreams come true.

So he did what any rational llama of science would do:

He packed slices of
emergency cake,
shimmied into his shiny
new time-travel pants—

and then went back in time to his birthday so that he could eat his birthday doughnut one more time.

TIME-TRAVEL PANTS:

But Llama did not know the first rule of time-travel pants. Llama had not read the instruction manual, so instead of traveling back to his birthday yesterday . . .

The MUST-READ INSTRUCTION MANUAL

It is your birthday

Llama *vorped* right past it.

Past the doughnut,

past yesterday,
past the past to—

LONG, LONG AGO

Llama had traveled back, long, long ago—

to a time of tubular hair, gnarly tunes,
and the most radical pants ever created.
His birthday doughnut was not here . . . no.

But something from this other time
called to Llama. Something familiar.

A *different* doughnut:
sweet and spectacular,
with extra, extra sprinkles.

Happy
Birthday

The doughnut looked lonely sitting there all alone, and Llama had a special place in his heart for lonely sweets. So Llama did the only thing he could think of to help the poor doughnut feel less lonely.

Llama had broken the second rule of time-travel pants. A rule not meant to be broken.

Never change (or eat) the past.

He had. He'd devoured every crumb and delicious sprinkle. He would pay dearly for it.

Filled with delight (and doughnut), Llama *vorped* back to the present without a care in the world.

Little did he know, someone followed him home.

TODAY
(AGAIN)

It was today (again), and Llama was face-to-face with a peculiar individual.

RUMBLE
RUMBLE
RUMBLE

Llama wasn't sure who this hungry-looking stranger was, but there was something about the shy baby llama that reminded him of past things he did not want to be reminded of.

Llama chose his next words very carefully:

Llama disliked strangers taking his name, but not as much as Llama disliked strangers taking his snacks.

Still, Llama was a gentleman.

So he made Baby Llama feel welcome.

He made Baby Llama a time-travel diaper.

And then . . . he made Baby Llama disappear.

But Baby Llama came back. (He was a quick learner.)

He came back again.

Again and again.

But each time Baby Llama came back, his time-travel diaper had an accident and brought back others.

They kept coming back.

TOMORROW

It was tomorrow, and tomorrows were Llama's spa days, but on this tomorrow, there would be no fuzzy slip-ees or lavender-scented bubbly baths . . .

Llama's house was a battleground of chaos. Prehistoric War-hogs laid siege to the cupboards. Buccaneer Bun-buns raided the cubbies and closets.

And in the party room, ancient Cave Llamas had started clubbing while futuristic Ro-pacas did the robot.

It was the worst dancing Llama had ever seen.
The past AND future looked grim.

Time was running out.

In a matter of minutes, Llama's house would be torn apart, his inventions smashed, his portraits mustache'd, and worst of all . . . his secret cake cellar would be ruined.

All that cake. Piles of cake. More
cake than any one Llama could ever lift.
He needed help . . . but could he trust
Baby Llama with his most precious sweets?

GURGLE

He could not.

Llama dashed for the cake. Baby Llama dashed for the cake.

I am Llama!

cried Llama, turning on his time-travel pants.

I am Llama!

repeated Baby Llama as he turned on his time-travel diaper.

But neither Llama nor Baby Llama had read the forty-second rule of time-travel pants . . .

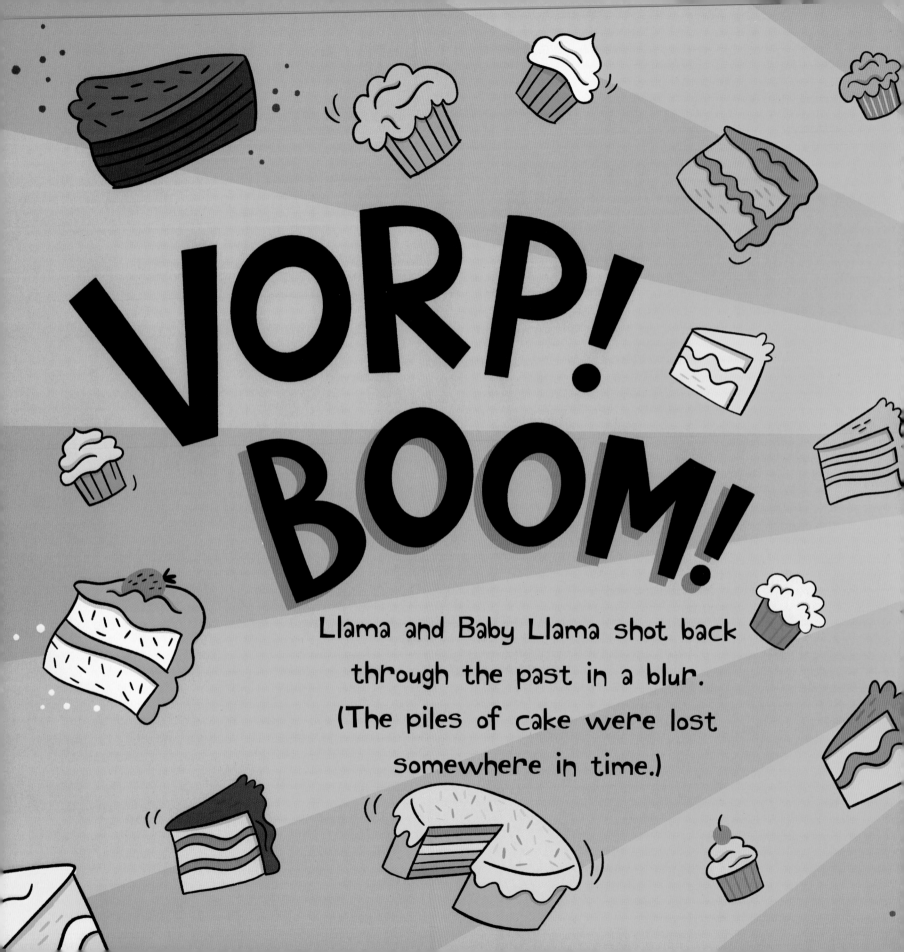

VORP! BOOM!

Llama and Baby Llama shot back
through the past in a blur.
(The piles of cake were lost
somewhere in time.)

LONG, LONG AGO (AGAIN)

Llama and Baby Llama found themselves long, long ago (again) . . . and Llama finally noticed something.

Something familiar.
Something sad and lonely that he had tried to forget before.
This party. The doughnut he shouldn't have devoured.
This face in front of him. All were his, from long, long ago.

Baby Llama was Llama, as a baby.
And as Llama looked at himself, he knew what
Baby Llama wanted, what *he* really wanted . . .

He knew what made sweet birthday treats the sweetest and
most spectacular. (And it wasn't extra sprinkles.)

So Llama made Baby Llama a fancy party hat.

Llama gave Baby Llama his slice of emergency chocolate cake.

"dat" said Llama.

"dat" repeated Baby Llama.

Now, Llama was many things:

A ROCK STAR.

A TEA CONNOISSEUR.

A SWASHBUCKLER OF THE HIGH SEAS.

But most of all, Llama was a llama of science. He knew that there were spectacular doughnuts—SPECTACULAR CAKES— out there, just waiting to be discovered . . .

IN THE FUTURE . . .

with his friends.